STORIES THE YEAR 'ROUND

I Don't Want to Melt

Alma Flor Ada

Illustrations by Vivi Escrivá

Translated from the Spanish by Rosa Zubizarreta

ALFAGUARA

INFANTIL Y JUVENIL

SANTILLANA

For Elaine Marie, for her beautiful presence in my life. And for Sarah, who is also an author.

© **1999 Santillana USA Publishing Co., Inc.**

2105 N.W. 86th Ave.
Miami, FL 33122

98 99 00 01 02 10 9 8 7 6 5 4 3 2 1

Printed in Mexico

ISBN: 1-58105-204-9

Alberto and Marcos finished placing their snowball on top of a larger one. Earlier, they had worked hard on the snowballs, smoothing them down until they were quite round and even. Now the boys looked over their work with satisfaction. It looked like a real snowman!

Right then Laura arrived.

"Look at what I've found!" she said as she held out a red woolen hat.

"Put this on him also," said Marcos as he took off the scarf he was wearing. "It got caught on a tree branch yesterday, and Mother said that she would buy me a new one."

In the wink of an eye, the snowman was wearing the hat and the scarf. He looked more and more like a little round man.

"He'll look even better if he's holding a broom," suggested Alberto. "I'll go and bring our old one. It's falling apart anyway."

And off he went to find the broom.

"He needs eyes," said Rafael, "and I know where I can find some." He ran to the garage.

A little while later, he returned with two very dark pieces of coal. When he put them on the snowman, the snowman was transformed. It seemed as though he really was looking out at the four children.

During the next few days, the snowman saw many things with his coal-black eyes. He saw how the children's mother came in and out of the house, her arms filled with packages. He also saw the children help her carry an enormous Christmas tree into the living room. And he enjoyed watching the glow of the colored tree lights reflected in the snow.

On Christmas Day, the snowman saw the children come outdoors with great big smiles on their faces and their new blue sleds in tow. He heard them shouting as they slid joyfully down the hill.

But only a few days later, the children were saying goodbye to him.

"See you later, Snowman!" Alberto called out.

"We're going to Miami to visit our grandmother," Laura explained.

"I'll bring you a coconut," said Marcos. "You'll be the only snowman in all of Detroit who has a coconut."

"We'll leave you this tray of birdseed. You can feed the birds and the squirrels and have them keep you company," said Laura.

"Wait for us, Snowman. We'll be back!" said Rafael. "And, whatever you do, don't melt!"

It was the first time that the snowman had ever heard the word "melt." And the truth is, although he didn't know what the word meant, he didn't like the sound of it at all.

He thought he might ask one of the birds or one of the squirrels who visited the yard more frequently now that the children weren't around. The little animals were very happy to come and eat the seeds and nuts that the children had left behind.

But as it turned out, he didn't have to ask.

A few days after the children left, the snowman woke up to a bright, sunny morning.

"I hope spring gets here soon," said one of the birds. "I love to see the trees all covered with flowers."

"And I love to eat acorns without having to dig them out from under the snow," added a squirrel.

"When all the snow is melted and gone, I'll be able to scratch the earth and find nice, fat, juicy worms to eat," said a robin.

"But why does snow melt?" the snowman was brave enough to ask.

The animals had never before heard the snowman speak. The squirrel, frightened, jumped onto the nearest tree trunk and did not stop running until she had reached a high branch. Then she stood very still, with her tail held high and her whiskers twitching. Meanwhile, all the birds had flown away.

But since the animals saw that the snowman did not move, nor try to scare them away with his broom, soon they all returned.

"Why does snow melt?" the snowman asked again.

"In springtime, the sun shines more strongly than it does in the winter," answered a robin.

"And the heat of the sun melts the snow," explained a squirrel.

"It's quite nice, really," said one of the sparrows. "Everything turns green, and there's lots of flowers and butterflies."

"And lots of good things to eat!" added a little mouse who had just joined the group.

"Does spring always come? Every single year?" asked the snowman.

"Yes, of course," said several birds at once.

"If we didn't know that springtime would soon come, winters would be horrible," added the little mouse.

"But . . . I don't want to melt!" cried the snowman.

All of the animals grew silent.

"It would be horrible to turn into a puddle of water," continued
the snowman. "And what would happen to my blue scarf, to my
red hat, and to my black eyes, if I turned into a puddle of water?"

The animals still didn't know what to say. Then a pair of doves who had overheard the conversation flew down from the branches of a nearby tree.

"Snow has to melt, so that all of the plants can grow," said the blue dove.

And the brown dove added, "No one can go against the ways of Nature. That's just how things are."

This time the snowman answered very quietly, "But I *really* don't want to melt!"

Although he spoke in a very low voice, the birds overheard him.

"When you melt, you'll turn into water. Then the water will flow until it finds a stream," said one of the robins.

"And then you'll travel until you reach a river or a lake," added the other robin.

"Maybe even until you reach the sea!" exclaimed one of the squirrels.

"And wherever that water goes, it will help plants grow, and help grow food for everyone," said the little mouse.

The snowman sighed. It was a long, deep sigh which blew several snowflakes up into the air.

"I really do like being a snowman. Are you sure that there's no way that I can keep from melting?"

There was so much sadness in his voice that all of the animals began to think.

"He's too big to fit inside a freezer," said a sparrow.

"Maybe he could go live in an ice-cream factory," suggested another sparrow.

"Or maybe he could go to the North Pole," proposed a squirrel.

"I have an idea," announced a robin. "Listen to this."

"I'll take care of your scarf," said the robin. "When it's time for you to melt, you can run off to see the world without any worries. Next winter, your scarf will be right here waiting for you."

"Your hat will be waiting for you, also," said the sparrows. "We'll be happy to take care of it for you."

"I'll take care of your eyes," said the squirrel. "They'll be perfectly safe in my squirrel hole."

"And we know just the place to hide your broom!" said the mice.

When the children got back from their vacation, they ran to greet the snowman.

True to his word, Marcos had brought back, not one, but several little coconuts. He placed them on the snowman as buttons.

"He's the best snowman in the whole neighborhood," said Alberto.

"He seems happy that we're back," said Laura.

Every day, when the children came home from school, they ran to greet the snowman.

And then, the month of March arrived.

"We have three days of vacation!" Alberto shouted happily.

"We're going on a trip with Mom," explained Marcos.

"Wait for us to get back," said Rafael. Then he added, "And please, try not to melt."

During the days that the children were away, the sun shone brightly. Each day, the snowman became smaller and the puddle by his feet grew larger.

Very early on the third morning, the animals gathered around the snowman.

"I'm taking your scarf," the robin announced gently.

"And we're taking your hat," said the sparrows.

"All of our cousins and uncles have come to help us carry the broom," said the mice.

"We'll take care of the coconuts," said the doves. "Though who would have ever thought of putting coconuts on a snowman?"

"I'll take your eyes," said the squirrel. "You won't need them for your travels around the world. I promise you that I will take very good care of them."

When the children returned that night, all that was left of the snowman was a puddle of water. But because they were very tired from their trip, the children did not notice a thing.

The next morning, Marcos encountered a robin who was very busily digging for worms in the grass. Alberto discovered that the tulips had started to bloom in the garden, and Laura smiled when she saw the first butterfly of the year.

Only Rafael looked around for the remains of the snowman. But when his sister and his brothers called for him to join them as they started on their way to school, Rafael went running after them.

That spring, the robin's nestlings
had a very warm blue nest, thanks to the
snowman's scarf. The baby sparrows were
not cold at all, huddled in their red nest
made out of the snowman's woolen hat.
The little squirrels went to sleep every
night listening to the story of the treasure
that was hidden underneath all of the
nuts and acorns stashed in the bottom of
the squirrel hole. The little mice, in turn,
never got tired of hearing about how it
had taken forty cousins and uncles to
carry the snowman's broom, which was
now hidden away underneath the nearby
bushes. And, as for the doves' nestlings,
they dreamed of flying to white sandy
beaches where tall coconut trees grew.

When summer arrived, the robins washed the scarf out in the creek. Then they hung it out to dry in the sun. The sparrows did the same with the wool hat.

The baby doves were already grown, and the little squirrels scampered about freely. It was very easy for them to become friends once they began to share what they knew about the snowman.

When the leaves began to turn red and fall from the trees, the little squirrels and the little mice did not have much time left to play any more. They were busy helping their parents gather and stockpile provisions for the long winter ahead.

"When will the first snow fall?" asked the baby sparrows.

The baby robins added, "We hope it's soon . . . we want to see what snow looks like."

Eventually the first snow did fall—not as soon as the children would have wanted it to, but much sooner than their parents did.

"Hurry up, it's getting dark," said Alberto, rolling a heap of snow into a huge ball.

"The head is almost ready," answered Marcos. "Why don't you help me lift it into place?"

"We're done!" said Laura, helping them lift the head onto the body of the snowman.

"Just in time for dinner!" said Rafael.

And as the other children headed into the house, he turned around and whispered, "Hello, Snowman!"

Once again, the animals gathered around the snowman in the early dawn.

"Here is your scarf," said the robins, wrapping it around his neck.

"And your wool hat," said the sparrows, as they placed it on the snowman's head.

"Here are your buttons," said the doves. "They've dried out a bit, but they're still good. Though who ever heard of a snowman with coconut buttons!"

"The whole family helped bring your broom," said the mice. "Eleven uncles and fifty-six cousins—a few more than last spring!"

"And here are your eyes," said the squirrels, as they placed them very carefully on his face.

"Thank you, my friends," said the snowman. "You were right when you told me that I didn't need to be afraid to melt. I saw some very interesting things as I traveled around the world."

The snowman told his animal friends how his waters had run to the creek, traveled to the Great Lakes, and then continued on downstream. He talked of the many ships that he had met along the way. He told of how he had fallen over huge waterfalls and turned into mist, and how he had finally reached the ocean. At last, he told how one summer day, when it was very hot, the little droplets of water had turned into vapor and floated up to become part of a cloud. It was very peaceful, floating around in the sky . . . and then, the day before yesterday, he had turned into snow, and fallen to earth once more.

On their way to school the next morning, the children were very surprised.

"But Mom said she didn't have the snowman's scarf and hat," said Laura.

"And look! She even kept the old broom!" said Alberto.

"My coconuts are a bit dried out," said Marcos, "I'll have to collect some new ones when we go to Miami again."

"Hello, Snowman!" said Rafael. As the others started on their way to school, he turned around and added, "I'd give anything to know all the places you've been since last spring!"